SPLINTER NO MORE

Written by Maureen Spurgeon
Illustrated by Clic Publishing

THERE was a deathly hush in the underground sewer. No sounds filtered down from the street, except for the occasional draught whistling through, then wailing into the darkness.

Footsteps echoed along the tunnel. The Teenage Mutant Hero Turtles hardly dared breathe. Their eyes were fixed on a strange-looking figure emerging from the shadows.

"He's here!" whispered Donatello.

"Yeah," breathed Raphael, "and he's brought..."

"The pizza!" finished Michaelangelo's voice from behind a huge pile of take-away boxes. "Flavour of the month - peanut butter and anchovies!"

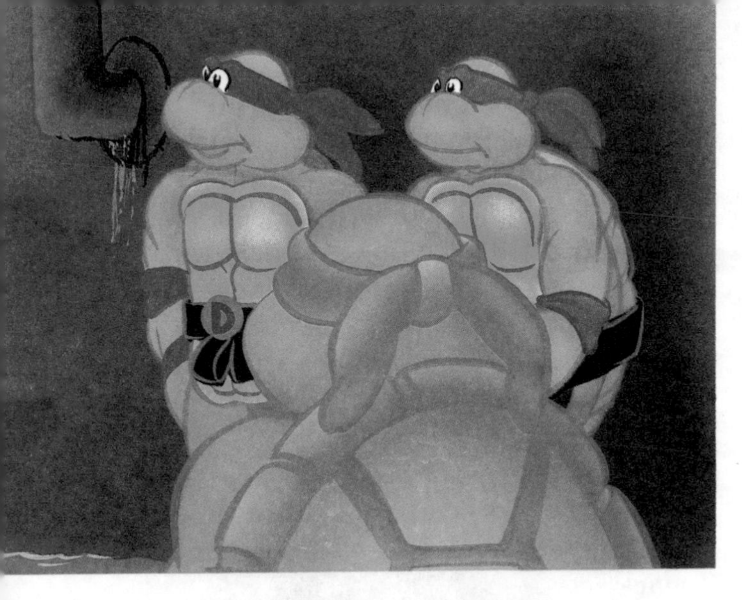

"Master Splinter!" he greeted the humanoid rat who had trained the Turtles in martial arts and given them their names. "How about some of your favourite fish?"

"Very thoughtful of you, Michaelangelo!" said Splinter with a deep sigh. "But I'm not hungry."

"Splinter's been acting mondo depressed lately," commented Michaelangelo to the others as Splinter turned away.

"Probably worried about Shredder's next move!" said Raphael, naming the enemy from Dimension X.

"I don't think that's it," said Leonardo thoughtfully. "I think Master Splinter misses being human!"

Donatello bolted down the last of his pizza and snapped his fingers. “Hold it, guys! I think I’ve got just the thing!”

He looked pleased with himself as he held up a jar filled with flakes of dried greenish gunk! The others were not impressed!

“This is what’s left of the mutagen goo that changed us from ordinary turtles into the half teenagers we are now - and changed Splinter into a mutant half-rat!” he explained.

“Aha!” cried Leonardo, getting the idea. “So maybe we can use it to change him back!”

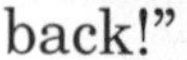

Each of them knew how Splinter was once the brilliant Japanese martial arts Professor Yoshi - until Shredder, in the disguise of a rival named Saki, had made him flee to America. Penniless, Yoshi had to live with the rats in an underground sewer - the same sewer where four unwanted turtles were dumped.

Now, hearing what the Turtles were saying, there was a new light in his eyes. "To be human, once more... To walk the streets, to feel the sunlight..." He paused. "As a rat, I have my night vision and my sense of smell."

"Yes," Leonardo broke in, "but as a human, you could go top-side at any time to see what Shredder's up to!"

They all gathered in Donatello's laboratory where they watched chemicals blending and changing colours, swirling through tubes and coils to a drip dispenser, making the radioactive goo glow and turn into liquid "Careful with that stuff, Donatello!"

murmured Raphael. "If we get any on us, it's back to the glass bowl in the pet shop!"

But Donatello was not their scientific genius for nothing! "Not to worry," he said, sucking up some of the goo into an atomizer spray.

The Turtles held their breath, and Splinter closed his eyes against the sudden, brilliant glow. Then, as it faded...

"Yoshi!" cried Donatello.

"It worked!" yelled Michaelangelo.

Yoshi was examining his hands in disbelief, and feeling his face. "I - I am human, once again! Thank you, Turtles!"

"Why don't you take your new body out for a road test?" grinned Raphael.

"Yes," Professor Yoshi smiled back. "Yes, I believe I will!"

Yoshi was still smiling when he climbed the ladder. Bright sunshine flooded the tunnel as he pushed back the cover leading to the street. Then, all was darkness. The Turtles were alone.

"He'll be back," said Leonardo, at last.

"Are you sure?" persisted Raphael. "I mean - he's human now."

"What if he wants to stay with his own kind?" Michaelangelo suggested huskily.

Leonardo swallowed hard. "It's his choice," he said.

Plenty was happening in New York that day - although it didn't seem like it to TV news-girl April O'Neil at Channel Six !

"Public Service Announcements for Library Week!" she snorted, consulting her clip-board. "What a boring..."

She stopped. Two peculiar-looking joggers were slinking through a door marked EMPLOYEES ONLY.

"Rocksteady and Bebop!" gasped April.

Nobody could mistake the punk semi-warthog and his rhino pal from Dimension X! And, wherever they went, the evil Shredder was never far away...

Leonardo was surprised when his Turtle-Com beeped and April's face appeared on the pocket video screen. "What is it, April?"

"I just saw Rocksteady and Bebop in the Public Library!" she told him.

The Turtles stood up, gaping at each other.

"Thanks, April!" said Leonardo. "We'll take it from here!"

To the Turtles, it seemed a wacky idea to be hounding Shredder in the public library! But that's just where he was, wearing a long, hooded robe that hid his steel helmet and visor.

"This is it!" he cried suddenly, his head bent over the pages of an old book. "The ancient spell that will open a portal to any Dimension!"

He clasped the precious pages. "No longer must I beg that pink-faced Krang's favours!" he went on, clearly enjoying this taste of power. "I can call my warriors from Dimension X on my own!"

Meanwhile, Yoshi was enjoying his taste of freedom!

"It's been so long since I've been able to walk among people," he said to himself, watching the crowds of tourists and busy New Yorkers in wonder.

And, what about the calm greenery of Central Park, he thought? He was looking forward to a quiet, peaceful stroll there!

It was very peaceful and quiet in the public library, too. So quiet, that Shredder could hear voices whispering in the corridor…

"April said she saw them go down this section..."

"The Turtles!" hissed Shredder. "Hide - quickly!" There was just time for him, Rocksteady and Bebop to dodge behind the nearest stacks of books, before the door creaked open.

"Mucho mysterioso…" murmured Michaelangelo.

"Shredder's been here!" whispered Leonardo. "I know it!"

"Wrong!" boomed Shredder, rising up from behind a pile of books. "I'm *still* here!"

He hurled a weapon at the largest book case in the room! There was an almighty explosion, and stacks of shelves and books crashed down on the heroes.

"What now, boss?" snorted Bebop.

Shredder did not notice a piece of paper fluttering to the ground. "Why," he said with an evil chuckle, "finish them, of course!"

Leonardo was first to recover. Seeing the two villains closing in, he scrambled to his feet - and, before Rocksteady or Bebop could do anything about it he whipped out his sword, hurling it at the radiator and slicing clean through the pipe!

"Hey!" Rocksteady and Bebop couldn't see a thing through the cloud of steam! "What's going on!"

The hissing and the warmth of the steam soon revived the other Turtles, Leonardo helping them to their feet.

"You really got them steamed, Leonardo!" grinned Raphael. He and Michaelangelo advanced towards the enemy.

"Yeah!" breathed Michaelangelo, the edge of his sharp sword glinting.

Panic-stricken, Rocksteady and Bebop made for the door, slamming it in the faces of the four Teenage Mutant Hero Turtles! It took quite a few seconds to untangle themselves from the four-way pile-up!

"Too bad they got away," said Leonardo, retrieving his sword. "We still have no idea what Shredder's up to!"

"Well, according to this," said Donatello, scanning the paper Shredder had dropped, "somewhere beneath the city, there's an old subway terminal that was once used as a temple by some weird cult!"

"So, what's Shredder going to do?" Raphael cut in. "Catch the train to Dimension X?"

"As a matter of fact," said Donatello, "yes!" He pointed a finger to show the others. "The temple is located at a point where different

Dimensions converge! If Shredder recites the spell at midnight, he can open a portal to any Dimension he wants!"

The Turtles viewed each other anxiously. They knew how much this could increase Shredder's power!

"We've got to stop him!" said Leonardo at last.

"But, how?" Raphael spread his flippers helplessly. "There are miles of old subway tunnels under this city!"

In the excitement they had almost forgotten the human Professor Yoshi. And Yoshi wasn't thinking about the Turtles, either. He was content to enjoy a pleasant stroll beside a little pond.

"Bad move, Pops," growled a voice behind him, "coming into the park by yourself!"

"But don't worry," someone else sniggered. "You won't live long enough to regret it!"

With three hefty-looking muggers closing in on him, it seemed like there was no escape! But, as Yoshi prepared to defend himself - the muggers reeled back in shock!

"What - what's happening?" stammered the first.

"He - he's..." the second one gulped, "he's turning into some kind of monster!"

Yoshi was relieved to see them running away. But, he was puzzled, too. What made them run? He certainly did feel strange. Then, he caught sight of his reflection in the pond and fell to his knees to make sure of what he was seeing. There was no mistake. His ears were once again large and pointed! A pink, hairless tail had sprouted behind him!

He scrambled to his feet. "The effects of Donatello's spray are wearing off!" he told himself. "I must get underground before I change completely!"

It so happened that Shredder was planning to go underground, too, and was tracing a route on the map with his finger.

"According to the old book," he mused, "the temple is - here! Now, I must translate the ancient spell which was used to open the portal! But, first..."

A slow smile spread across Shredder's face as he reached for the Com-Link. He quite enjoyed seeing Krang's disembodied pink-blob face appearing on the screen!

"What is it this time, Shredder?"

"I have found the Key to Other Realms!" replied the smug villain.

"Oh, really!" retorted Krang. "Well, if you expect me to have your foot warriors all ready to go, you can forget it!"

"I - I'll show you!" Shredder started to bluster. "I'll open a portal to Dimension X, tonight!"

"I'd advise you to be careful," said Krang smoothly. "Unless the spell is spoken quite correctly, it could open a gate to yet another Dimension. And there are Dimensions much worse than this one!"

While all this was going on, April had been busy. She was writing up the Library Week Report when her Turtle-Com started bleeping.

"Sorry to call you at the office," came Michaelangelo's voice, "but this is mondo important!"

"Didn't you do a documentary on old subway tunnels a few weeks ago?" asked Donatello. "We need a video tape of it!"

"Okay!" she hissed, keeping an eye on nosey-parker Irma at the front desk. "Can do!"

"Great!" cried Leonardo. "Meet us at the Cornelius Building!"

They had no idea that Shredder was already on his way there, with the book containing the ancient spell in one hand and the map in the other.

"We're getting close to the temple!" he told Rocksteady and Bebop.

"Glad to hear it, boss!" grunted Bebop, clutching his stun laser. "These tunnels give me the creeps!"

"Dunno how the Turtles can live down here!" added Rocksteady.

"The Turtles!" Shredder burst out. "I had forgotten they live in the sewers!"

He pressed the button on his Com-Link, waiting impatiently for Krang's pink face to appear.

"I need you to send me the neuroscrambler I invented! he gabbled. "I can set it to produce a brain-warping frequency that will cause the Turtles to see each other as enemies!"

"Well…" Krang hesitated.

Shredder cut in impatiently. "While the Turtles are fighting each other, I will open the portal to Dimension X!"

"It's against my better judgement!" said Krang, turning his robot body towards the main control panel inside the huge Technodrome. "But, all right!"

"Thank you, Krang! You will not regret this!"

And, Yoshi? The only thing on his mind was to escape the angry mob which were chasing him with loud cries. "Give humans something different from themselves," he panted to himself, "and they find something to hate!"

"There he is!" bellowed one policeman.

"He's heading for the subway!" roared another.

Yoshi could see there was nowhere to run - only the platform and the railway tracks. His one chance was to jump down, pressing his body up against the wall of the platform.

"Whatever that thing is," came the policeman's voice, booming strangely through the emptiness, "it looks dangerous!"

Yoshi held his breath, a beam from the policeman's torch barely missing him. Then came something more frightening - the rumble of a distant train, getting louder and louder...

April and the Turtles couldn't hear any trains where they were. And they couldn't see much, either!

"According to April's video," Donatello kept saying, "that old underground temple is right here!"

Suddenly, he stopped. A low, throbbing hum seemed to be sending him off balance.

"Hey, guys... I feel kinda weird..."

"Yeah - me too!" said Raphael. "My brain hurts!"

April could see that Michaelangelo was affected as well, the way he was stumbling and falling around.

"Hey!" Raphael bawled, drawing his sword. "Watch where you're going, nerd!"

To April's astonishment, Donatello raised his wooden Japanese *bo* in self defence. "Who are you calling a nerd?"

"Cut it out, fellas!" Leonardo broke in wearily - but Michaelangelo made a grab at

him, ignoring the look of horrified disbelief on April's face.

"Shut up, geek! You're getting too big for your shell!"

"Why are you doing this?" she pleaded. "What's happening?"

Further along the tunnel, the policemen had finally given up hounding Yoshi - except that he wasn't Yoshi any longer. As the two men turned away and headed back up the stairs, a brown,furry head rose above the edge of the platform. Splinter did not really need to see himself mirrored in a chocolate machine.

"Once again, Yoshi is gone," he mused sadly, "and only Splinter remains." He gave a deep sigh. "So be it." And he leapt down into the tunnel - not too far from the spot where April was trying to break up the pitched battle between the four Turtles.

"Have you all gone crazy?" she shouted desperately. "What would Splinter think if he saw you?"

A fierce blow from Michaelangelo sent Leonardo reeling back. April noticed him shaking his head, as if he were trying to collect his thoughts. Even his words were spoken with an effort. "April's right... We - must - not - fight - each - other..."

Nobody said anything - which meant that April could hear the strange humming noise coming from the wall.

"That weird sound..." she said. "That must be what's causing it!"

It wasn't hard to find Shredder's neuroscrambler, hidden in the wall!

"I was right!" cried April, throwing it into the air. "Get it, guys!" The Teenage Mutant Hero Turtles were a team again. They hurled up their weapons and hit Shredder's neuroscrambler at exactly the same moment.

"Mondo nutziness!" stated Michaelangelo, still a bit dazed. "Thanks, April!"

"Gee," said Donatello, "it's just like Master Splinter saved us again, even though he's no longer part of us."

"You said it, Donatello!" sighed Leonardo. "Come on, guys!"

By now, Bebop and Rocksteady were wishing they were back on Dimension X! Or in the public library. Anywhere, away from the endless maze of tunnels!

"We been looking for hours, Boss!" whined Bebop.

"We're never gonna find this temple!" groaned Rocksteady, as they rounded yet another curve. But then they stopped short, their mouths gaping wide open.

"You were saying?" said Shredder triumphantly. His eyes gleamed. The light of glowing crystals mounted in wall brackets picked out details of the decorated tiles and the altar flanked by carved columns, and tall pillars rising up to the roof.

Shredder lit the incense remaining in one of the burners, and there was a blaze of light. It cast long, dark shadows as he stepped to the altar, turning the yellowing pages of the ancient book. And if he heard any sound - like the long, sensitive nose of a rat sniffing at the strong smell of incense - he was past caring. It was nearly midnight. Time to begin the all-powerful spell! Nothing else mattered.

"All right, Shredder!" a voice rang through the network of tunnels. "Your number is up!"

"The Turtles!" Shredder's eyes narrowed.

"Now!" he yelled to Rocksteady and Bebop. Shouts and cries of pain echoed and re-echoed around the deserted temple as the two villains began firing their stun lasers, until April and the Turtles collapsed in a heap.

"Congratulations!" sniggered Shredder, taking their weapons. "You're just in time to witness my hour of triumph. Too bad it's the last thing you'll ever see!"

He returned to the altar, glancing up at

the clock on the wall. Midnight, at last!

"By ancient lore and powers dark," began Shredder, reading from the book, "Let space and time begin to part!"

At this point, Master Splinter emerged from the the tunnel. His eyes widened in horror at the sight of a three-dimensional portal shimmering into existence between the pillars!

"Portal, now open wide!" continued Shredder. "Reveal at last what is inside!"

Now the portal was a solid door way. The flames from the incense burners fluttered and bent in the wind which blew into the opening.

"Key within to my success, Bridge the gap to Dimension..."

"Stop!"

Shredder whirled around to face Splinter, not seeing that the portal door was opening wider to reveal a black, dead-looking landscape criss-crossed with jagged cracks and bottomless pits. Its sky hung low and dark.

"No!" screamed out Shredder, following

Master Splinter's horrified gaze.

"No! The spell has been mis-cast!"

"Master Splinter!" cried Leonardo, seeing Rocksteady and Bebop reaching for their stun lasers. "Look out!"

His warning came just in time. Somehow, Splinter managed to dodge the ray-blasts, giving Donatello the chance to kick out and knock Bebop off his feet! Rocksteady came back on the attack - but once Leonardo had snatched up the stun laser, it was easy to flip the punk rhino over his head with it!

"Whoo-aa-hh!" screamed Rocksteady, seeing a huge tentacle rise up from one of the cracks in the black landscape. It snaked its way through the portal, grabbing Shredder and coiling around him! More tentacles rose up, this time snatching Rocksteady, Bebop - and April!

"What's going on?" demanded Donatello.

"Shredder's opened a portal to the wrong Dimension!" explained Master Splinter.

"So instead of Dimension X," put in Raphael, "Shredder's tuned into Dimension X-Y-Z!"

More and more of the monster was appearing every minute, groping forward with even more tentacles, and trying to squeeze its horrible, slimy bulk through the portal!

"The portal will only remain open for a few minutes," announced Master Splinter. "Once it closes, that creature will remain in our world!"

"We've got to drive it back through the portal!" shouted Leonardo.

With cries of "Turtle Power!" the Turtles went on an all-out attack! The trouble was, whenever a tentacle was cut, it promptly grew back, stronger than ever! Their one triumph belonged to Raphael, when he stabbed at the tentacle holding April. Instinctively it drew away, releasing her. But Michaelangelo had barely pulled her to safety before the wound healed and the tentacle started groping around again!

It seemed Shredder was reluctant to lose Bebop and Rocksteady, as well! He hurled two explosives that each burst on the tentacles which held the partners in crime. They were thrown free - but still the monster kept on growing!

"It's coming through the portal!" yelled Donatello.

"Quick!" shouted Leonardo, keeping his cool, as always. "Lure it towards the columns!" He ran and stood in front of one of the columns, ducking away from the tentacle which lashed out towards him. So, instead of hitting the brave Turtle leader, it smashed through the column, bringing

down a hail of masonry! With a roar, the monster turned its attention to Donatello, standing firm before another column. And, as a tentacle whipped towards him, he used his Japanese wooden *bo* to pole-vault out of the way!

Crash! Down came another column, broken in two by the monster! Loud creaks and groans were coming from the roof. Cracks appeared which became wider and wider. Then the remaining columns started to crumble and the whole temple began to cave in!

"Uh-oh!" cried Michaelangelo, through clouds of dust and smoke. "Time to boogie"

It was clear that the monster was thinking along the same lines! With stonework and masonry falling all around, it retreated back, almost at the same instant the portal shrank to a tiny dot - and disappeared.

The Turtles barely had time to jump back down into the tunnel, before the entire building collapsed with a final earth-shattering rumble.

"Thanks for your help, April!" said Donatello, after it was all over.

"Don't mention it!" April gave a long-suffering smile. "I love spending a relaxing evening fighting monsters from other Dimensions!"

Later, there were pizzas for the Turtles - and time to welcome back their friend, Master Splinter.

"Gee, Master," said Donatello sadly, "we're really sorry the experiment to change you back into a human didn't take!"

Splinter smiled. "I do not regret it. After seeing how humans treat one another, I prefer being an animal."

"Besides," he went on in his deep, wise voice, "if I had not returned to my present form, I would not have been able to reach you in time - and Shredder would have won!"

"I never thought of it that way," said Leonardo.

Michaelangelo said nothing. He was remembering something else Master Splinter had told them, long, long ago…

Do not speak when your mouth is full of your favourite peanut butter and anchovy pizza!